Baby
Business

Mittie Cuetara

Dutton Children's Books · New York

For Sam, Stewie, big and little Dan, and the Hurths.
Thanks, you guys!

CIP Data is available.

Published in the United States by Dutton Children's Books,
a division of Penguin Putnam Books for Young Readers
345 Hudson Street, New York, New York 10014
www.penguinputnam.com

Designed by Tim Hall
Manufactured in China
First Edition
ISBN 0-525-47026-3
10 9 8 7 6 5 4 3 2 1

Contents

Waking · 6

Breakfast · 7

Walking · 8

Dressing · 9

Crawling · 10

Sports · 11

Ailing · 12

Entertainment · 13

Screaming · 14

Visitors · 15

Swinging · 16

Snacking · 17

Playing · 18

Pooping · 19

Toys · 20

Naptime · 21

Music · 22

Car Ride · 23

Books · 24

Midnight · 25

Brotherly Love · 26

Bathtime · 27

Bedtime · 28

Sleeping · 29

Waking

Morning baby in my bed,
Soft and warm as new-made bread.
Must you rise SO early, Ned?
Bright-eyed little baby

Breakfast

Marcus drops and spills and throws,
Covers everybody's clothes.
Time for clean-up—get the hose!
Messy little baby

Walking

One step, two steps, what a thrill!
One more step and down goes Jill.
Wait, she's up—and at it still.
Spunky little baby

Dressing

Jane does not know WHAT to wear,
And furthermore, she doesn't care.
She's happiest completely bare.
Naked little baby

Crawling

Nellie's just learned how to crawl—
Zips away and down the hall.
Hear her frantic parents call.
Speedy little baby

Sports

Baby Andrew tries and tries
To catch those bugs and butterflies,
Getting baby exercise.
Active little baby

Ailing

Billie isn't feeling right—
Stuffy nose, no appetite.
Keeps her parents up all night.
Crabby little baby

Entertainment

Zacky loves those silly faces.

Doesn't care for social graces.

Puts the grown-ups through their paces.

Jolly little baby

Screaming

Tess and Emma love to scream.
Babies need to let off steam.
See those baby tonsils gleam!
Noisy little babies

Visitors

Aaron doesn't really care
Whether Mommy's friends are there.
Doesn't see why HE should share.
Demanding little baby

Swinging

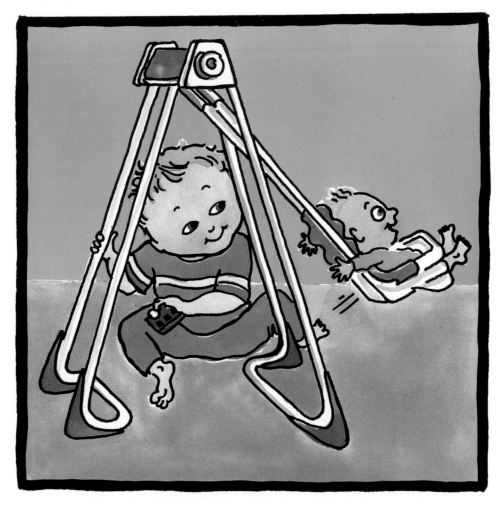

Listen to Katrina sing
In her automatic swing.
This is baby's favorite thing.
Dizzy little baby

Snacking

Gum and string and bits of wax—
Gaby sees them all as snacks.
Mom and Dad have heart attacks.
Hungry little baby

Playing

Nancy loves to play, but she
Drives her brother up a tree.
Mom and Dad must referee.
Rascal little baby

Pooping

Eddie's awful quiet there.
What's that odor in the air?
Someone's diaper needs repair.
Stinky little baby

Toys

Malcolm's toy box overflows
With proper toys his parents chose.
But grown-up toys are best, he knows.
Wily little baby

Naptime

Nappy-time for little Jake,
Even though he's wide awake.
Nap is for his mommy's sake.
Wiggly little baby

Music

Sam and Sara love to pound,
And though they make a joyous sound,
It's sometimes hard to be around.
Booming little babies

Car Ride

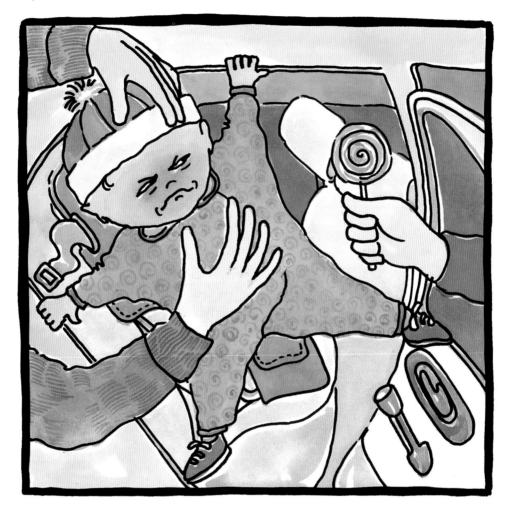

"I will not go!" screams little Pete.
"They will not get me in that seat!"
But given time, and something sweet . . .
Stubborn little baby

Books

Books are great, thinks little Steve,
Fun to chew or climb or heave.
Loves the bookstore, hates to leave.
Literary baby

Midnight

Baby Phoebe naps all day—
Up at midnight, wants to play.
Parents' nerves begin to fray.
Frisky little baby

Brotherly Love

Baby Ted admires Lou,
Robot wars, and homework too.
Oh, the things that big boys do.
Devoted little baby

Bathtime

Alexander loves a scrub,
Then a fuzzy-towel rub.
Tiny ring around the tub.
Yummy little baby

Bedtime

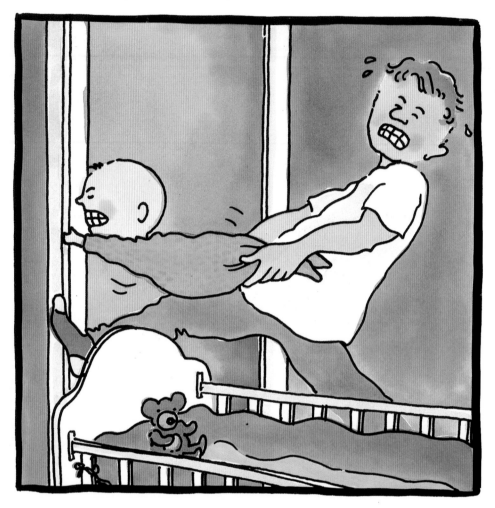

Daniel hates to say good night,
Daniel isn't ready quite.
He can sure put up a fight!
Feisty little baby

Sleeping

Bathed and changed and dressed and fed,
Snuggled up with Frog and Ted,
Stewie's finally gone to bed.
Good night, little baby

The End